Pigs Will Be Pigs

Fun with Math and Money

story by Amy Axelrod

pictures by Sharon McGinley-Nally

Aladdin Paperbacks

The Pigs were hungry…again.
"Let's have a snack," suggested
Mr. Pig. "Dear, what do we have to eat?"

Mrs. Pig opened the refrigerator. "Oh no! It's empty! And I just went grocery shopping this morning! Who ate up all the food?" she asked.

"B. J., Dave, and Mike helped us," said the piglets, "and Dad raided the refrigerator a few times."

"No problem," said Mr. Pig. "Let's go out to eat."

"Great idea," said Mrs. Pig, "except for one thing."

"What's that?" asked Mr. Pig.

"I didn't get to the bank and I don't have any money," she said. "Do you?"

Mr. Pig opened his wallet. "All I have is a dollar, and that's certainly not enough to feed the Pigs. Children, how about you? Any money?"

The piglets shook their heads no.

"Well, family," said Mrs. Pig, "there's only one thing to do."

" Hunt for

money! "

"Let's start with the bedrooms upstairs," said Mr. Pig.
He looked through all the closets and drawers. "Look
what I found," Mr. Pig said to Mrs. Pig. "That lucky
two-dollar bill I was saving. It was in with my socks."

Mrs. Pig searched the beds, looked under the carpet, in the night table, and in her jewelry box.

"Not too much here," she said to Mr. Pig. "Mostly a lot of dust. But I did find two nickels, five pennies, and one quarter."

Meanwhile, the piglets were busy hunting in their room. They found six shiny dimes at the bottom of their toy chest and a one-dollar bill in the bookshelf. Then they sat down to count out their penny collection....They counted two hundred pennies.

"Back downstairs, family!" said Mr. Pig.

Mrs. Pig and the piglets opened the front hall closet. They checked coat pockets and all of Mrs. Pig's pocketbooks. They found four quarters, ten dimes, one fifty-cent piece, and seventeen pennies.

The Pigs were on a roll. Mrs. Pig checked the laundry room and found a wet five-dollar bill. Mr. Pig looked through the kitchen cupboards and pantry. "Dear," he said to his wife, "there's nothing in here. I'm going down to the basement."

A few minutes later, Mr. Pig came
running up from the basement holding a
twenty-dollar bill.

"Look what I found in my toolbox!" he said. "It's time to eat!"

Mrs. Pig put all of the money in a shoe box. She counted it several times while Mr. Pig drove the family to their favorite restaurant.

When they arrived at the restaurant the Pigs said to the waitress, "We're the Pigs and we're very hungry. What's the special?"

APPETIZERS

Nacho chips with salsa $ 1.50

Stuffed jalapeños $ 2.00

EGG DISHES

Huevos rancheros
ranch-style eggs
(tortillas topped with fried eggs,
spicy chili sauce, grated cheese,
and sliced avocado) $ 2.99

Migas
scrambled eggs with tostado
(eggs scrambled with pieces of
crispy tortilla, tomato, fried
pepper, onion, and garlic) $ 2.99

All egg dishes served with
green-chili corn bread.

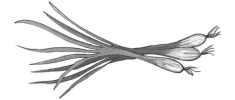

SOUPS

Black bean
Cup $ 1.25
Bowl $ 2.25

Chef's special
(a hearty soup of potato, cheese,
and green chilis)

Cup $ 2.00
Bowl $ 3.00

SALADS

Salad bar
Make your own tostados—top
crispy tortillas with black beans,
chili sauce, grated cheese,
chopped tomatoes, and lettuce.
Finish with sour cream.

With dinner $ 1.99
Salad bar only $ 2.99

Taco salad
(mixed green salad with spicy
dressing in a crispy tortilla bowl)
$ 2.99

Tax and tip included

TORTILLA SPECIALTIES

Cheese enchiladas
(3 corn tortillas filled with cheese
and red chili sauce—served with
southwestern rice) $ 4.99

Guacamole enchiladas
(3 corn tortillas filled with
guacamole and green chili
sauce—served with
southwestern rice) $ 4.99

Bean burritos
(3 flour tortillas wrapped
around frijoles refritos and
grated cheese—served with
southwestern rice) $ 4.99

Chimichangas
(3 deep-fried bean burritos
topped with salsa and
guacamole—served with
southwestern rice) $ 4.99

MEXICAN PIZZA

Large $ 3.99
Small $ 2.99

SIDE DISHES

Colache
southwestern succotash
(string beans, corn, tomatoes,
summer squash, and hot green
chilis) $ 3.00

Calavacitas
(summer squash, corn, onions,
garlic, and chilis) $ 3.00

Quelites
(spinach and pinto beans with
scallions, garlic, and chilis) $ 3.00

Texas caviar
(marinated black-eyed peas) $ 1.50

Frijoles refritos
(refried pinto beans) $ 1.50

DESSERTS

Sopaipillas
deep-fried honey puffs $ 2.00

Flan
custard $ 1.50

Biscochitos
Mexican cookies $ 1.50

Natillas
islands of meringue on custard
$ 2.50

Deep-fried ice cream
(chocolate or vanilla) $ 2.00

Fresh mango/papaya $ 2.00

BEVERAGES

Cola   glass $ .75
    pitcher $ 2.00

Frozen delight
(strawberry or mango) $ 2.25

Mexican coffee $ 1.00

Regular coffee $ 1.00

Tea $ .75

TODAY'S SPECIAL

Cup of chef's special soup

Combo of:

    1 cheese enchilada
    1 guacamole enchilada
    1 chimichanga

(served with southwestern rice
and green-chili corn bread)

Unlimited visits
to our salad bar

Coconut smoothie

Sopaipillas or
deep-fried ice cream

Coffee/tea

ALL FOR ONLY $ 7.99
Tax and tip included

The Pigs ordered four specials. They ate and ate until they could eat no more. They paid the bill, then left for home.

"Boy, am I stuffed!" said Mr. Pig as he parked the car in the driveway. "I can't button my pants."

"I know what you mean," said Mrs. Pig. "I feel like I'm going to explode."

"We have bellyaches," said the piglets.

"Just a few more steps and we'll be at the front door," said Mrs. Pig. "Then we can all relax in our nice, clean, neat, cozy house. There's nothing like home, sweet home."

"Your mother's right, kids," said Mr. Pig.
"There's nothing like home, sweet…"

How much money did the Pigs find on their hunt?

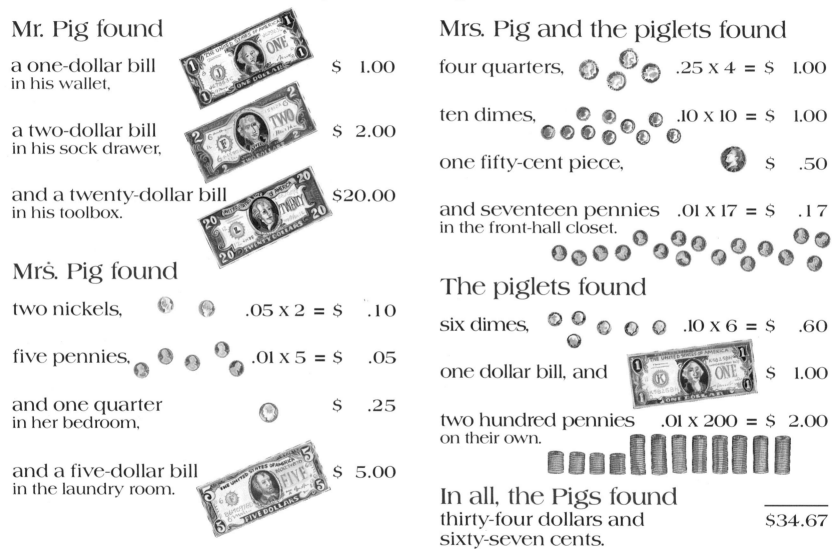

Mr. Pig found

a one-dollar bill
in his wallet, $ 1.00

a two-dollar bill
in his sock drawer, $ 2.00

and a twenty-dollar bill
in his toolbox. $20.00

Mrs. Pig found

two nickels,   .05 x 2 = $ .10

five pennies,   .01 x 5 = $ .05

and one quarter
in her bedroom, $ .25

and a five-dollar bill
in the laundry room. $ 5.00

Mrs. Pig and the piglets found

four quarters,   .25 x 4 = $ 1.00

ten dimes,   .10 x 10 = $ 1.00

one fifty-cent piece, $ .50

and seventeen pennies   .01 x 17 = $ .17
in the front-hall closet.

The piglets found

six dimes,   .10 x 6 = $ .60

one dollar bill, and $ 1.00

two hundred pennies   .01 x 200 = $ 2.00
on their own.

In all, the Pigs found
thirty-four dollars and   _____
sixty-seven cents. $34.67

How much money did the Pigs spend at the Enchanted Enchilada?
How much money do the Pigs have left?

Bonus question: Can you order other meals for the Pigs from the
Enchanted Enchilada menu? Remember they have $34.67 to spend!

For Michael, Bram, and David,
with all my love

—A.A.

...for friends through thick and thin—
Cupid, Elle, Diane, Ginny, Heidi, Irma, Iva,
Kathie, Lillian, Linda, Nancy, Pat, Shannon,
Virginia, and Wendy. Thank you, sisters!

—S.M.-N.

25 Years of Magical Reading

ALADDIN PAPERBACKS
EST. 1972

First Aladdin Paperbacks edition September 1997   Text copyright © 1994 by
Amy Axelrod   Illustrations copyright © 1994 by Sharon McGinley-Nally   Aladdin
Paperbacks   An imprint of Simon & Schuster Children's Publishing Division   1230
Avenue of the Americas   New York, NY 10020   All rights reserved, including the
right of reproduction in whole or in part in any form.   Also available in a Simon &
Schuster Books for Young Readers edition.   Designed by Christy Hale   The text
of this book is set in American Classic Bold.   The illustrations are rendered in
inks, watercolors, and acrylics.   Printed and bound in the United States of
America   10 9 8 7 6 5 4 3 2 1   The Library of Congress has cat-
aloged the hardcover edition as follows: Axelrod, Amy. Pigs will be pigs / story
by Amy Axelrod ; pictures by Sharon McGinley-Nally.   p.   cm. Summary: The
hungry Pig family learns about money and buying power as they turn the house
upside down looking for enough money to buy dinner at the local restaurant.   ISBN
0-02-765415-X   1. Pigs—Fiction. (1. Money—Fiction. 2. Finance, Personal—Fiction.)
I. McGinley-Nally, Sharon, ill. II. Title.   PZ7.A96115Pi 1994 [E]—dc20 93-7640
ISBN 0-689-81219-1 (Aladdin pbk.)